A Gift

A Gift
Yong Chen

BOYDS MILLS PRESS

HONESDALE, PENNSYLVANIA

Thanks to Dongdong Chen, Ph.D., Department of Asian Studies,
Seton Hall University, for his assistance.

Boyds Mills Press, Inc.
815 Church Street
Honesdale, Pennsylvania 18431
Printed in China

CIP data is available

First edition
The text of this book is set in 16-point Berkeley Book.
The illustrations are done in watercolor.

10 9 8 7 6 5 4 3 2 1

To my wife and family, who are the source of my inspiration
—Y.C.

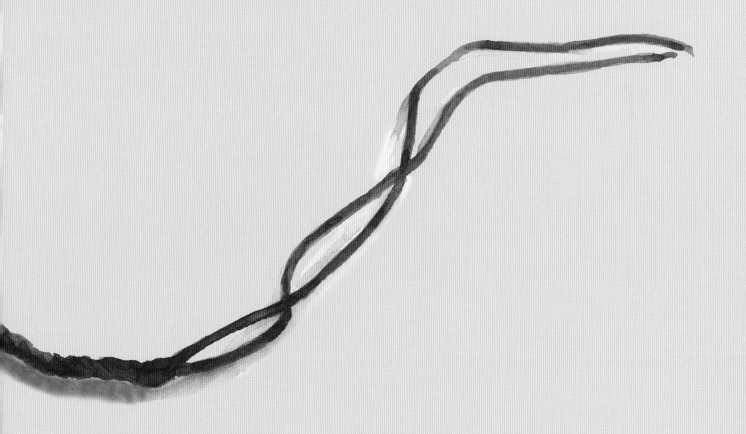

Homesick.

That's how Amy's mother feels whenever it's Chinese New Year. She thinks about her brothers and her sister, who live on the other side of the world.

Amy has never met her uncles and her aunt, but she knows a lot about them.

Uncle Zhong is a farmer.

Uncle Ming is a fisherman.

Aunt Mei is a nurse who works in the local hospital.

They think about Amy's mother, too.

Sometimes they send letters
about their lives in China.
Sometimes they send packages,
like the one delivered today.

Amy and her mother opened the box
that had traveled so far.

Inside, they found a letter.

Our Dear Sister,
Last month, Zhong was working in his field.

His plow unearthed a beautiful stone.

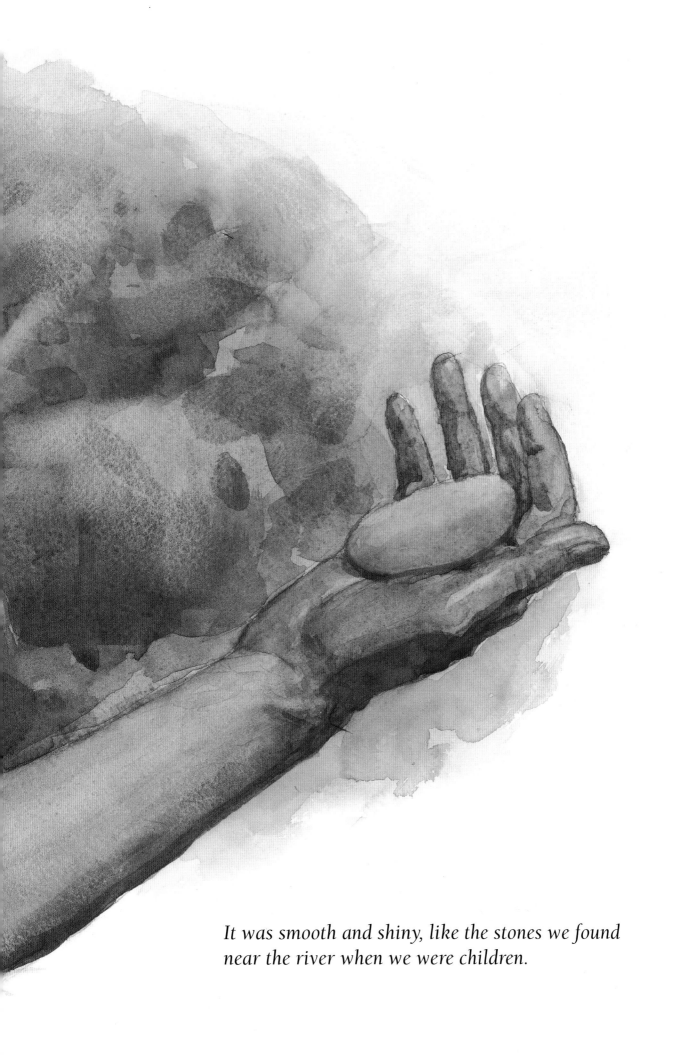

It was smooth and shiny, like the stones we found near the river when we were children.

In the evening, Zhong brought the stone to town.

He showed it to Ming, who looked at the stone
and saw a dragon hidden inside.

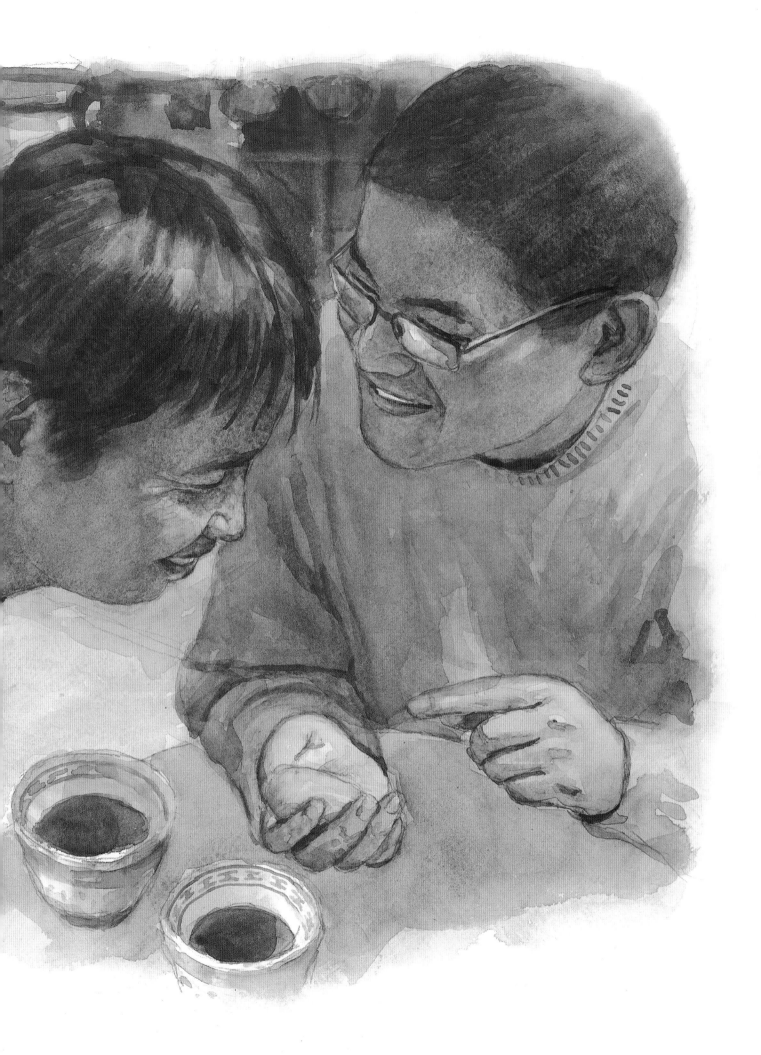

Ming worked for many days, carving and polishing,
until he brought the dragon out of the stone.

Today, Ming showed me what he had created.
The stone that Zhong had found in the field is now a necklace for Amy.
We hope she likes it.

Happy New Year.
Your sister,
Mei

"This is for you, sweetheart,"
said Amy's mother. "It's a gift from our family."
"A dragon!" said Amy.

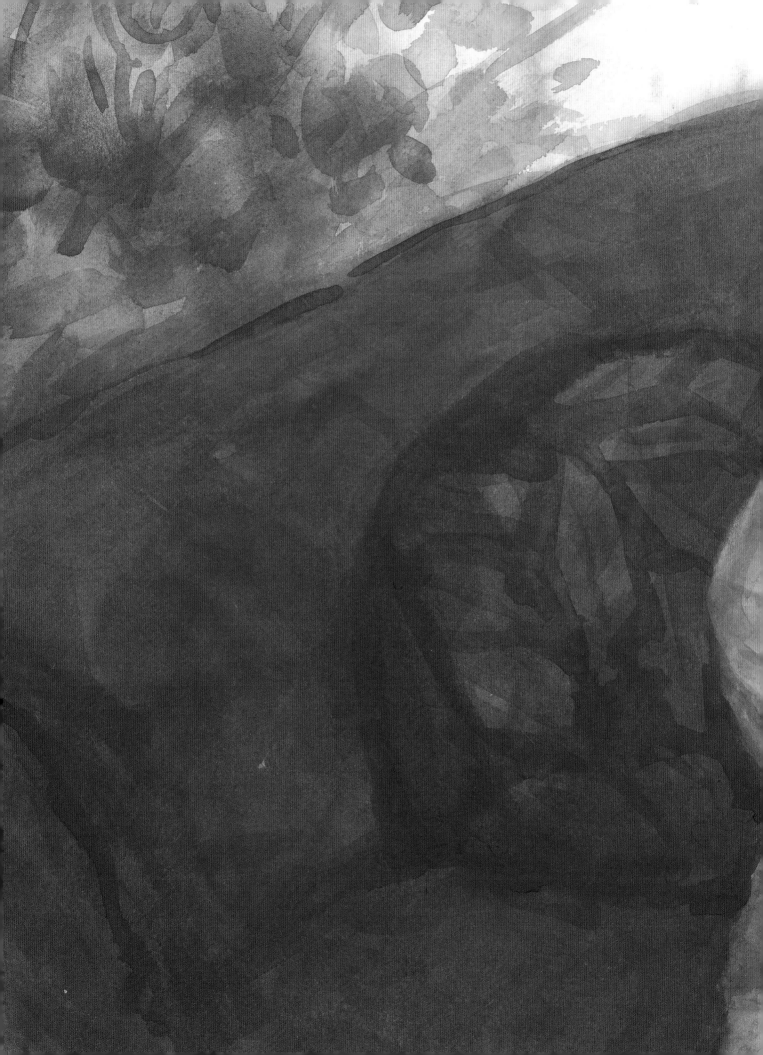

"The dragon is the symbol of China,"
said Amy's mother. "Happy New Year!"
    "Happy New Year to you, too!" said Amy.
"And to my family far away."

Author's Note

Chinese New Year is the most important holiday in the Chinese culture. It is celebrated by Chinese all over the world. During this festive occasion, families and friends visit with one another in a practice called "new-year visits."

Millions of people of Chinese birth or descent live outside of China. To stay in touch with their families, they exchange letters, talk by telephone, and send gifts, like the one in this story.

The dragon necklace given to Amy is made out of a stone from the motherland and represents a piece of home.

Originally the symbol of the emperor of China, the dragon later became the symbol of China itself. Sometimes the Chinese people call themselves "descendants of the dragon."

In the Chinese tradition, red is the color of luck. Using a red string for the necklace expresses love and a wish for good fortune.

—Y.C.